Samuel Johnson

The Prince of Abissinia

A Tale: Vol. I.

Samuel Johnson

The Prince of Abissinia
A Tale: Vol. I.

ISBN/EAN: 9783337120313

Printed in Europe, USA, Canada, Australia, Japan

Cover: Foto ©Andreas Hilbeck / pixelio.de

More available books at **www.hansebooks.com**

THE

PRINCE

OF

ABISSINIA.

A

TALE.

IN TWO VOLUMES.

VOL. I.

LONDON:

Printed for R. and J. Dodsley, in Pall-Mall;
and W. Johnston, in Ludgate-Street.
MDCCLIX.

CONTENTS

OF THE

FIRST VOLUME.

A 2   CHAP.

CHAP. IV.

CHAP. V.

CHAP. VI.

CHAP. VII.

CHAP. VIII.

CHAP. IX.

CHAP.

CONTENTS.

CHAP. X.

CHAP. XI.

CHAP. XII.

CHAP. XIII.

CHAP. XIV.

CHAP.

C H A P.

CHAP. XX.

CHAP. XXI.

CHAP. XXII.

CHAP. XXIII.

CHAP. XXIV.

CHAP.

CHAP. XXV.

THE

THE

HISTORY

OF

RASSELAS,

PRINCE OF ABISSINIA.

CHAP. I.

Defcription of a palace in a valley.

YE who liften with credulity to the whifpers of fancy, and purfue with eagernefs the phantoms of hope; who expect that age will perform the promifes of youth, and that the deficien-

cies of the prefent day will be fupplied
by the morrow ; attend to the hiftory of
Raffelas prince of Abiffinia.

Raffelas was the fourth fon of the
mighty emperour, in whofe dominions the Father of waters begins his
courfe; whofe bounty powers down the
ftreams of plenty, and fcatters over half
the world the harvefts of Egypt.

According to the cuftom which has
defcended from age to age among the
monarchs of the torrid zone, he was confined in a private palace, with the other
fons and daughters of Abiffinian royalty,
till the order of fucceffion fhould call him
to the throne.

The place, which the wifdom or policy of antiquity had deftined for the refidence of the Abiffinian princes, was a
fpa-

fpacious valley in the kingdom of Amhara, furrounded on every fide by mountains, of which the fummits overhang the middle part. The only paffage, by which it could be entered, was a cavern that paffed under a rock, of which it has long been difputed whether it was the work of nature or of human induftry. The outlet of 'the cavern was concealed by a thick wood, and the mouth which opened into the valley was clofed with gates of iron, forged by the artificers of ancient days, fo maffy that no man could, without the help of engines, open or fhut them.

From the mountains on every fide, rivulets defcended that filled all the valley with verdure and fertility, and formed a lake in the middle inhabited by fifh of every fpecies, and frequented by every

fowl

fowl whom nature has taught to dip the wing in water. This lake difcharged its fuperfluities by a ftream which entered a dark cleft of the mountain on the northern fide, and fell with dreadful noife from precipice to precipice till it was heard no more.

The fides of the mountains were co-vered with trees, the banks of the brooks were diverfified with flowers; every blaft fhook fpices from the rocks, and every month dropped fruits upon the ground. All animals that bite the grafs, or broufe the fhrub, whether wild or tame, wandered in this extenfive circuit, fe-cured from beafts of prey by the moun-tains which confined them. On one part were flocks and herds feeding in the paf-tures, on another all the beafts of chafe frifk-

frifking in the lawns; the fpritely kid was bounding on the rocks, the fubtle monkey frolicking in the trees, and the folemn elephant repofing in the fhade. All the diverfities of the world were brought together, the bleffings of nature were collected, and its evils extracted and excluded.

The valley, wide and fruitful, fupplied its inhabitants with the neceffaries of life, and all delights and fuperfluities were added at the annual vifit which the emperour paid his children, when the iron gate was opened to the found of mufick; and during eight days every one that re-fided in the valley was required to pro-pofe whatever might contribute to make feclufion pleafant, to fill up the vacan-cies of attention, and leffen the tediouf-

nefs

nefs of time. Every defire was immediately granted. All the artificers of
pleafure were called to gladden the fefti-
vity; the muficians exerted the power of
harmony, and the dancers fhewed their
activity before the princes, in hope that
they fhould.pafs their lives in this blisful
captivity, to which thefe only were admitted whofe performance was thought able
to add novelty to luxury. Such was
the appearance of fecurity and delight
which this retirement afforded, that they
to whom it was new always defired that it
might be perpetual; and as thofe, on
whom the iron gate had once clofed,
were never fuffered to return, the effect
of longer experience could not be known.
Thus every year produced new fchemes
of delight, 'and new competitors for im-
prifonment.

The

The palace ftood on an eminence raifed about thirty paces above the furface of the lake. It was divided into many fquares or courts, built with greater or lefs magnificence according to the rank of thofe for whom they were' defigned. The roofs were turned into arches of maffy ftone joined with a cement that grew harder by time, and the building ftood from century to century, deriding the folftitial rains and equinoctial hurricanes, without need of reparation.

This houfe, which was fo large as to be fully known to none but fome ancient officers who fucceffively inherited the fecrets of the place, was built as if fufpicion herfelf had dictated the plan. To every room there was an open and fecret paffage, every fquare had a communica-

tion

tion with the reft, either from the upper
ftories by private galleries, or by fubterranean paffages from the lower apartments. Many of the columns had un-
fufpected cavities, in which fucceffive
monarchs repofited their treafures. They
then clofed up the opening with marble,
which was never to be removed but in the
utmoft exigencies of the kingdom; and
recorded their accumulations in a book
which was itfelf concealed in a tower
not entered but by the emperour, attended by the prince who ftood next in
fucceffion.

C H A P.

CHAP. II.

The difcontent of Raffelas in the happy valley.

HERE the fons and daughters of Abiffinia lived only to know the foft viciffitudes of pleafure and repofe, attended by all that were fkilful to delight, and gratified with whatever the fenfes can enjoy. They wandered in gardens of fragrance, and flept in the fortreffes of fecurity. Every art was practifed to make them pleafed with their own condition. The fages who inftructed them, told them of nothing but the miferies of publick life, and defcribed all beyond the mountains as regions of calamity,

lamity, where difcord was always rag-
ing, and where man preyed upon man.

To heighten their opinion of their
own felicity, they were daily entertained
with fongs, the fubject of which was the
happy valley. Their appetites were excited by frequent enumerations of different enjoyments, and revelry and merriment was the bufinefs of every hour from
the dawn of morning to the clofe of
even.

Thefe methods were generally fucceff-
ful; few of the princes had ever wifhed
to enlarge their bounds, but paffed their
lives in full conviction that they had all
within their reach that art or nature could
beftow, and pitied thofe whom fate had
excluded from this feat of tranquility, as
the

the fport of chance, and the flaves of mifery.

Thus they rofe in the morning, and
lay down at night, pleafed with each
other and with themfelves, all but Raffelas, who, in the twenty-fixth year
of his age, began to withdraw himfelf
from their paftimes and affemblies, and
to delight in folitary walks and filent meditation. He often fat before tables co-
vered with luxury, and forgot to tafte
the dainties that were placed before him :
he rofe abruptly in the midft of the fong,
and haftily retired beyond the found of
mufick. His attendants obferved the
change and endeavoured to renew his love
of pleafure : he neglected their endeavours, repulfed their invitations, and
fpent day after day on the banks of rivulets

vulets sheltered with trees, where he
sometimes listened to the birds in the
branches, sometimes observed the fish
playing in the stream, and anon cast his
eyes upon the pastures and mountains
filled with animals, of which some were
biting the herbage, and some sleeping
among the bushes.

This singularity of his humour made
him much observed. One of the Sages,
in whose conversation he had formerly
delighted, followed him secretly, in hope
of discovering the cause of his disquiet.
Rasselas, who knew not that any one
was near him, having for some time
fixed his eyes upon the goats that were
brousing among the rocks, began to compare their condition with his own.

" What,"

" What," faid he, " makes the diffe-
rence between man and all the reft of the
animal creation? Every beaft that ftrays
befide me has the fame corporal neceffi-
ties with myfelf; he is hungry and crops
the grafs, he is thirfty and drinks the
ftream, his thirft and hunger are ap-
peafed, he is fatisfied and fleeps; he rifes
again and is hungry, he is again fed and
is at reft. I am hungry and thirfty like
him, but when thirft and hunger ceafe
I am not at reft; I am, like him, pained
with want, but am not, like him, fatif-
fied with fulnefs. The intermediate
hours are tedious and gloomy; I long
again to be hungry that I may again
quicken my attention. The birds peck
the berries or the corn, and fly away to
the groves where they fit in feeming happinefs on the branches, and wafte their
lives

lives in tuning one unvaried feries of founds. I likewife can call the lutanift and the finger, but the founds that pleafed me yefterday weary me to day, and will grow yet more wearifome to morrow. I can difcover within me no power of perception which is not glutted with its proper pleafure, yet I do not feel myfelf delighted. Man has furely fome latent fenfe for which this place affords no gratification, or he has fome defires diftinct from fenfe which muft be fatisfied before he can be happy."

After this he lifted up his head, and feeing the moon rifing, walked towards the palace. As he paffed through the fields, and faw the animals around him, " Ye, faid he, are happy, and need not envy me that walk thus among you, burthened

thened with myself; nor do I, ye gentle beings, envy your felicity ; for it is not the felicity of man. I have many dif- tresses from which ye are free ; I fear pain when I do not feel it ; I sometimes shrink at evils recollected, and some- times start at evils anticipated : surely the equity of providence has ballanced peculiar sufferings with peculiar enjoy- ments."

With observations like these the prince amused himself as he returned, uttering them with a plaintive voice, yet with a look that discovered him to feel some complacence in his own perspicacity, and to receive some solace of the miseries of life, from consciousness of the delicacy with which he felt, and the eloquence with which he bewailed them. He min-

gled

gled cheerfully in the diverſions of the
evening, and all rejoiced to find that his
heart was lightened.

C H A P. III.

The wants of him that wants nothing.

ON the next day his old inſtructor,
imagining that he had now made
himſelf acquainted with his diſeaſe of
mind, was in hope of curing it by coun-
ſel, and officiouſly ſought an opportunity
of conference, which the prince, having
long conſidered him as one whoſe intellects
were exhauſted, was not very willing to
afford : " Why, ſaid he, does this man
thus intrude upon me ; ſhall I be never

suffuffered to forget thofe lectures which pleafed only while they were new, and to become new again muft be forgotten?" He then walked into the wood, and com-pofed himfelf to his ufual meditations; when, before his thoughts had taken any fettled form, he perceived his perfuer at his fide, and was at firft prompted by his impatience to go haftily away; but, be-ing unwilling to offend a man whom he had once reverenced and ftill loved, he invited him to fit down with him on the bank.

The old man, thus encouraged, be-gan to lament the change which had been lately obferved in the prince, and to en-quire why he fo often retired from the pleafures of the palace, to lonelinefs and filence. " I fly from pleafure, faid the prince, becaufe pleafure has ceafed to pleafe; I am lonely becaufe I am miferable, and am unwilling to cloud with my prefence the happinefs of others."

"You, Sir, faid the fage, are the firft who has complained of mifery in the *happy valley*. I hope to convince you that your complaints have no real caufe. You are here in full poffeffion of all that the emperour of Abiffinia can beftow; here is neither labour to be endured nor danger to be dreaded, yet here is all that labour or danger can procure. Look round and tell me which of your wants is without fupply: if you want nothing, how are you unhappy?"

"That I want nothing, faid the prince, or that I know not what I want, is the caufe of my complaint; if I had any
known

known want, I fhould have a certain wifh; that wifh would excite endeavour, and I fhould not then repine to fee the fun move fo flowly towards the weftern mountain, or lament when the day breaks and fleep will no longer hide me from myfelf. When I fee the kids and the lambs chafing one another, I fancy that I fhould be happy if I had fomething to perfue. But, poffeffing all that I can want, I find one day and one hour exactly like another, except that the latter is ftill more tedious than the former. Let your experience inform me how the day may now feem as fhort as in my childhood, while nature was yet frefh, and every moment fhewed me what I never had obferved before. I have already enjoyed too much; give me fomething to defire."

The old man was furprifed at this new fpecies of affliction, and knew not what to reply, yet was unwilling to be filent., " Sir, faid he, if you had feen the miferies of the world, you would know how to value your prefent ftate." " Now, faid the prince, you have given me fomething to defire; I fhall long to fee the miferies of the world, fince the fight of them is neceffary to happinefs."

C H A P.   IV.

The prince continues to grieve and mufe.

AT this time the found of mufick proclaimed the hour of repaft, and the converfation was concluded. The

old

old man went away fufficiently difcon-
tented to find that his reafonings had`
produced the only conclufion which they
were intended to prevent. But in the
decline of life fhame and grief are of
fhort duration ; whether it be that we
bear eafily what we have born long, or
that, finding ourfelves in age lefs regarded, we lefs regard others ; or, that we
look with flight regard upon afflictions,
to which we know that the hand of death
is about to put an end.

The prince, whofe views were extended to a wider fpace, could not fpeedily
quiet his emotions. He had been before terrified at the length of life which
nature promifed him, becaufe he confidered that in a long time much muft be
endured ; he now rejoiced in his youth,

be-

becaufe in many years much might be done.

This firft beam of hope, that had been ever darted into his mind, rekindled youth in his cheeks, and doubled the luftre of his eyes. He was fired with the defire of doing fomething, though he knew not yet with diftin&tnefs, either end or means.

He was now no longer gloomy and unfocial; but, confidering himfelf as mafter of a fecret ftock of happinefs, which he could enjoy only by concealing it, he affe&ted to be bufy in all fchemes of diverfion, and endeavoured to make others pleafed with the ftate of which he himfelf was weary. But pleafures ne-ver can be fo multiplied or continued,

as

as not to leave much of life unemployed; there were many hours, both of the night and day, which he could fpend without fufpicion in folitary thought. The load of life was much lightened: he went eagerly into the affemblies, becaufe he fuppofed the frequency of his prefence neceffary to the fuccefs of his purpofes; he retired gladly to privacy, becaufe he had now a fubject of thought.

His chief amufement was to picture to himfelf that world which he had never feen; to place himfelf in various conditions; to be entangled in imaginary difficulties, and to be engaged in wild adventures: but his benevolence always terminated his projects in the relief of diftrefs, the detection of fraud, the de-

feat

feat of oppreſſion, and the diffuſion of happineſs.

Thus paſſed twenty months of the life of Raſſelas. He buſied himſelf ſo intenſely in viſionary buſtle, that he forgot his real ſolitude ; and, amidſt hourly preparations for the various incidents of human affairs, neglected to conſider by what means he ſhould mingle with mankind.

One day, as he was ſitting on a bank, he feigned to himſelf an orphan virgin robbed of her little portion by a treacherous lover, and crying after him for reſtitution and redreſs. So ſtrongly was the image impreſſed upon his mind, that he ſtarted up in the maid's defence, and run forward to ſeize the plunderer with all

all the eagernefs of real perfuit. Fear naturally quickens the flight of guilt. Raffelas could not catch the fugitive with his utmoft efforts; but, refolving to weary, by perfeverance, him whom he could not furpafs in fpeed, he preffed on till the foot of the mountain ftopped his courfe.

Here he recollected himfelf, and fmiled at his own ufelefs impetuofity. Then raifing his eyes to the mountain, " This, faid he, is the fatal obftacle that hinders at once the enjoyment of pleafure, and the exercife of virtue. How long is it that my hopes and wifhes have flown beyond this boundary of my life, which yet I never have attempted to furmount! "

Struck

Struck with this reflection, he fat down to mufe, and remembered, that fince he firft refolved to efcape from his confinement, the fun had paffed twice over him in his annual courfe. He now felt a degree of regret with which he had never been before acquainted. He confidered how much might have been done in the time which had paffed, and left nothing real behind it. He compared twenty months with the life of man. " In life, faid he, is not to be counted the ignorance of infancy, or imbecility of age. We are long before we are able to think, and we foon ceafe from the power of acting. The true period of human exiftence may be reafonably eftimated as forty years, of which I have mufed away the four and twentieth part. What I have loft was certain, for I have certainly

certainly poſſeſſed it; but of twenty months to come who can aſſure me ? "

The conſciouſneſs of his own folly pierced him deeply, and he was long before he could be reconciled to himſelf. " The reſt of my time, ſaid he, has been loſt by the crime or folly of my anceſtors, and the abſurd inſtitutions of my country ; I remember it with diſguſt, but without remorſe : but the months that have paſſed ſince new light darted into my ſoul, ſince I formed a ſcheme of reaſonable felicity, have been ſquandered by my own fault. I have loſt that which can never be reſtored : I have ſeen the ſun riſe and ſet for twenty months, an idle gazer on the light of heaven : In this time the birds have left the neſt of their mother, and committed themſelves to the woods and to the fkies: the kid has forfaken the teat, and learned by degrees to climb the rocks in queft of independant fuftenance. I only have made no advances, but am ftill helplefs and ignorant. The moon, by more than twenty changes, admonifhed me of the flux of life; the ftream that rolled before my feet upbraided my inactivity. I fat feafting on intellectual luxury, regardlefs alike of the examples of the earth, and the inftructions of the planets. Twenty months are paft, who fhall reftore them!"

These forrowful meditations faftened upon his mind; he paft four months in refolving to lofe no more time in idle refolves, and was awakened to more vigorous exertion by hearing a maid,

who

who had broken a porcelain cup, remark, that what cannot be repaired is not to be regretted.

This was obvious ; and Raffelas reproached himfelf that he had not difcovered it, having not known, or not confidered, how many ufeful hints are obtained by chance, and how often the mind, hurried by her own ardour to diftant views, negleĉts the truths that lie open before her. He, for a few hours, regretted his regret, and from that time bent his whole mind upon the means of efcaping from the valley of happinefs.

CHAP.

C H A P. V.

The prince meditates his efcape.

HE now found that it would be very difficult to effect that which it was very eafy to fuppofe effected. When he looked round about him, he faw himfelf confined by the bars of nature which had never yet been broken, and by the gate, through which none that once had paffed it were ever able to return. He was now impatient as an eagle in a grate. He paffed week after week in clambering the mountains, to fee if there was any aperture which the bufhes might conceal, but found all the fummits inacceffible by their prominence. The iron

gate

gate he defpaired to open ; for it was not only fecured with all the power of art, but was always watched by fucceffive fentinels, and was by its pofition expofed to the perpetual obfervation of all the inhabitants.

He then examined the cavern through which the waters of the lake were difcharged ; and, looking down at a time when the fun fhone ftrongly upon its mouth, he difcovered it to be full of broken rocks, which, though they permitted the ftream to flow through many narrow paffages, would ftop any body of folid bulk. He returned difcouraged and dejeɛted; but, having now known the bleffing of hope, refolved never to defpair.

In

In thefe fruitlefs fearches he fpent ten months. The time, however, paffed cheerfully away : in the morning he rofe with new hope, in the evening applaud- ed his own diligence, and in the night flept found after his fatigue. He met a thoufand amufements which beguiled his labour, and diverfified his thoughts. He difcerned the various inftincts of ani- mals, and properties of plants, and found the place replete with wonders, of which he purpofed to folace himfelf with the contemplation, if he fhould never be able to accomplifh his flight; re- joicing that his endeavours, though yet unfuccefsful, had fupplied him with a fource of inexhauftible enquiry.

But his original curiofity was not yet abated; he refolved to obtain fome knowledge

ledge of the ways of men. His wifh
ftill continued, but his hope grew lefs.
He ceafed to furvey any longer the walls
of his prifon, and fpared to fearch by new
toils for interftices which he knew could
not be found, yet determined to keep his
defign always in view, and lay hold on
any expedient that time fhould offer.

C H A P. VI.

A differtation on the art of flying.

AMONG the artifts that had
been allured into the happy valley, to labour for the accommodation and
pleafure of its inhabitants, was a man
eminent for his knowledge of the mechanick powers, who had contrived ma-

ny engines both of ufe and recreation.
By a wheel, which the ftream turned, he
forced the water into a tower, whence
it was diftributed to all the apartments of
the palace. He erected a pavillion in.the
garden, around which he kept the air
always cool by artificial fhowers. One
of the groves, appropriated to the ladies,.
was ventilated by fans, to which the rivulet that run through it gave a conftant
motion; and inftruments of foft mufick
were placed at proper diftances, of which
fome played by the impulfe of the wind,
and fome by the power of the ftream.

This artift was fometimes vifited by
Raffelas, who was pleafed with every
kind of knowledge, imagining that the
time would come when all his acquifitions
fhould be of ufe to him in the open world.

He

He came one day to amufe himfelf in his ufual manner, and found the mafter bufy in building a failing chariot: he faw that the defign was practicable upon a level furface, and with expreffions of great efteem folicited its completion. The workman was pleafed to find himfelf fo much regarded by the prince, and refolved to gain yet higher honours. "Sir, faid he, you have feen but a fmall part of what the mechanick fciences can perform. I have been long of opinion, that, inftead of the tardy conveyance of fhips and chariots, man might ufe the fwifter migration of wings; that the fields of air are open to knowledge, and that only ignorance and idlenefs need crawl upon the ground."

D 2　　　　This

This hint rekindled the prince's defire of paffing the mountains ; and having feen what the mechanift had already per-formed, he was willing to fancy that he could do more ; yet refolved to enquire further before he fuffered hope to afflict him by difappointment. " I am afraid, faid he to the artift, that your imagina-tion prevails over your fkill, and that you now tell me rather what you wifh than what you know. Every animal has his element affigned him ; the birds have the air, and man and beafts the earth." " So, replied the mechanift, fifhes have the water, in which yet beafts can fwim by nature, and men by art. He that can fwim needs not defpair to fly : to fwim is to fly in a groffer fluid, and to fly is to fwim in a fubtler. We are only to pro-portion our power of refiftance to the

dif-

different denfity of the matter through which we are to pafs. You will be neceffarily upborn by the air, if you can renew any impulfe upon it, fafter than the air can recede from the preffure."

" But the exercife of fwiming, faid the prince, is very laborious ; the ftrongeft limbs are foon wearied ; I am afraid the act of flying will be yet more violent, and wings will be of no great ufe, unlefs we can fly further than we can fwim."

" The labour of rifing from the ground, faid the artift, will be great, as we fee it in the heavier domeftick fowls ; but, as we mount higher, the earth's attraction, and the body's gravity, will be gradually diminifhed, till we fhall arrive at

D 3   a

a region where the man will float in
the air without any tendency to fall : no
care will then be neceffary, but to move
forwards, which the gentleft impulfe
will effect. You, Sir, whofe curiofity
is fo extenfive, will eafily conceive with
what pleafure a philofopher, furnifhed
with wings, and hovering in the fky, would
fee the earth, and all its inhabitants, rolling beneath him, and prefenting to
him fucceffively, by its diurnal motion,
all the countries within the fame parallel.
How muft it amufe the pendent fpecta-
tor to fee the moving fcene of land and
ocean, cities and defarts! To furvey
with equal fecurity the marts of trade,
and the fields of battle ; mountains in-
fefted by barbarians, and fruitful regions
gladdened by plenty, and lulled by
peace! How eafily fhall we then trace
the

the Nile through all his paffage; pafs over to diftant regions, and examine the face of nature from one extremity of the earth to the other!"

" All this, faid the prince, is much to be defired, but I am afraid that no man will be able to breathe in thefe regions of fpeculation and tranquility. I have been told, that refpiration is difficult upon lofty mountains, yet from thefe precipices, though fo high as to produce great tenuity of the air, it is very eafy to fall : and I fufpect, that from any height, where life can be fupported, there may be danger of too quick defcent."

" Nothing, replied the artift, will ever be attempted, if all poffible objections muft be firft overcome. If you will fa-

your

vour my project I will try the firft flight at
my own hazard. I have confidered the
ftructure of all volant animals, and find
the folding continuity of the bat's wings
moft eafily accommodated to the human
form. Upon this model I fhall begin
my tafk to morrow, and in a year expect
to tower into the air beyond the malice or
purfuit of man. But I will work only
on this condition, that the art fhall not
be divulged, and that you fhall not re-
quire me to make wings for any but
ourfelves."

" Why, faid Raffelas, fhould you envy others fo great an advantage ? All
fkill ought to be exerted for univerfal
good ; every man has owed much to
others, and ought to repay the kindnefs
that he has received."

"If

" If men were all virtuous, returned
the artift, I fhould with great alacrity
teach them all to fly.   But what would
be the fecurity of the good, if the bad
could at pleafure invade them from the
fky ?   Againft an army failing through
the clouds neither walls, nor mountains,
nor feas, could afford any fecurity.   A
flight of northern favages might hover
in the wind, and light at once with irre-
fiftible violence upon the capital of a
fruitful region that was rolling under
them.   Even this valley, the retreat of
princes, the abode of happinefs, might
be violated by the fudden defcent of fome
of the naked nations that fwarm on the
coaft of the fouthern fea."

The prince promifed fecrecy, and waited for the performance, not wholly hope-
                                        lefs

lefs of fuccefs. He vifited the work from time to time, obferved its progrefs, and remarked the ingenious contrivances to facilitate motion, and unite levity with ftrength. The artift was every day more certain that he fhould léave vultures and eagles behind him, and the contagion of his confidence feized upon the prince.

In a year the wings were finifhed, and, on a morning appointed, the maker appeared furnifhed for flight on a little promontory : he waved his pinions a while to gather air, then leaped from his ftand, and in an inftant dropped into the lake. His wings, which were of no ufe in the air, fuftained him in the water, and the prince drew him to land, half dead with terrour and vexation.

CHAP.

C H A P. VII.

The prince finds a man of learning.

THE prince was not much afflicted
by this difafter, having fuffered
himfelf to hope for a happier event, only becaufe he had no other means of efcape
in view. He ftill perfifted in his defign
to leave the happy valley by the firft
opportunity.

His imagination was now at a ftand;
he had no profpect of entering into the
world; and, notwithftanding all his endeavours to fupport himfelf, difcontent
by degrees preyed upon him, and he began again to lofe his thoughts in fadnefs,

when

when the rainy feafon, which in thefe countries is periodical, made it inconvenient to wander in the woods.

The rain continued longer and with more violence than had been ever known: the clouds broke on the furrounding mountains, and the torrents ftreamed into the plain on every fide, till the cavern was too narrow to difcharge the water. The lake overflowed its banks, and all the level of the valley was covered with the inundation. The eminence, on which the palace was built, and fome other fpots of rifing ground, were all that the eye could now difcover. The herds and flocks left the paftures, and both the wild beafts and the tame retreated to the mountains.

This

This inundation confined all the princes to domeſtick amuſements, and the
attention of Raſſelas was particularly
ſeized by a poem, which Imlac re-
cited, upon the various conditions of
humanity. He commanded the poet
to attend him in his apartment, and re-
cite his verſes a ſecond time; then
entering into familiar talk, he thought
himſelf happy in having found a man
who knew the world ſo well, and could
ſo ſkilfully paint the ſcenes of life. He
aſked a thouſand queſtions about things,
to which, though common to all other
mortals, his confinement from childhood
had kept him a ſtranger. The poet pitied his ignorance, and loved his curioſity, and entertained him from day to
day with novelty and inſtruction, ſo that
the prince regretted the neceſſity of ſleep,
and

and longed till the morning fhould renew his pleafure.

As they were fitting together, the
prince commanded Imlac to relate
his hiftory, and to tell by what accident
he was forced, or by what motive
induced, to clofe his life in the happy valley. As he was going to begin
his narrative, Raffelas was called to a
concert, and obliged to reftrain his curiofity till the evening.

C H A P. VIII.

The hiftory of Imlac.

THE clofe of the day is, in the regions of the torrid zone, the only
feafon of diverfion and entertainment,
and

and it was therefore mid-night before the mufick ceafed, and the princeffes retired. Raffelas then called for his companion and required him to begin the ftory of his life.

" Sir, faid Imlac, my hiftory will not be long: the life that is devoted to knowledge paffes filently away, and is very little diverfified by events. To talk in publick, to think in folitude, to read and to hear, to inquire, and anfwer inquiries, is the bufinefs of a fcholar. He wanders about the world without pomp or terrour, and is neither known nor valued but by men like himfelf.

" I was born in the kingdom of Goiama, at no great diftance from the fountain of the Nile. My father was a wealthy

thy merchant, who traded between the inland countries of Africk and the ports of the red fea. He was honeſt, frugal and diligent, but of mean fentiments, and narrow comprehenſion : he deſired only to be rich, and to conceal his riches, leſt he ſhould be fpoiled by the governours of the province.".

" Surely, ſaid the prince, my father muſt be negligent of his charge, if any man in his dominions dares take that which belongs to another. Does he not know that kings are accountable for injuſtice permitted as well as done ? If I were emperour, not the meaneſt of my fubjects ſhould be oppreffed with impunity. My blood boils when I am told that a merchant durſt not enjoy his honeſt gains for fear of loſing by the rapacity

of

of power. Name the governour who robbed the people, that I may declare his crimes to the emperour."

" Sir, said Imlac, your ardour is the natural effect of virtue animated by youth : the time will come when you will acquit your father, and perhaps hear with lefs impatience of the governour. Oppreffion is, in the Abiffinian dominions, neither frequent nor tolerated ; but no form of government has been yet dif-covered, by which cruelty can be whol-ly prevented. Subordination fuppofes power on one part and fubjection on the other ; and if power be in the hands of men, it will fometimes be abufed. The vigilance of the fupreme magiftrate may do much, but much will ftill re-main undone. He can never know all the crimes that are committed, and can feldom punifh all that he knows."

" This, faid the prince, I do not understand, but I had rather hear thee than difpute. Continue thy narration."

" My father, proceeded Imlac, originally intended that I fhould have no other education, than fuch as might qualify me for commerce; and difcovering in me great ftrength of memory, and quicknefs of apprehenfion, often declared his hope that I fhould be fome time the richeft man in Abiffinia."

" Why, faid the prince, did thy father defire the increafe of his wealth, when it was already greater than he durft difcover or enjoy? I am unwilling to
doubt

doubt thy veracity, yet inconfiftencies cannot both be true."

" Inconfiftencies, anfwered Imlac, cannot both be right, but, imputed to man, they may both be true. Yet diverfity is not inconfiftency. My father might expect a time of greater fecurity. However, fome defire is neceffary to keep life in motion, and he, whofe real wants are fupplied, muft admit thofe of fancy."

" This, faid the prince, I can in fome meafure conceive. I repent that I inter-rupted thee."

" With this hope, proceeded Imlac, he fent me to fchool; but when I 'had once found the delight of knowledge,

E 2 and

and felt the pleafure of intelligence and the pride of invention, I began filently to defpife riches, and determined to difappoint the purpofe of my father, whofe groffnefs of conception raifed my pity. I was twenty years old before his tendernefs would expofe me to the fatigue of travel, in which time I had been inftructed, by fucceffive mafters, in all the literature of my native country. As every hour taught me fomething new, I lived in a continual courfe of gratifications; but, as I advanced towards manhood, I loft much of the reverence with which I had been ufed to look on my inftructors; becaufe, when the leffon was ended, I did not find them wifer or better than common men.

" At

" At length my father refolved to ini-
tiate me in commerce, and, opening one
of his fubterranean treafuries, counted
out ten thoufand pieces of gold. This,
young man, faid he, is the ftock with
which you muft negociate. I began with
lefs than the fifth part, and you fee
how diligence and parfimony have in-
creafed it. This is your own to wafte
or to improve. If you fquander it by ne-
gligence or caprice, you muft wait for
my death before you will be rich : if, in
four years, you double your ftock, we
will thenceforward let fubordination
ceafe, and live together as friends and
partners; for he fhall always be equal
with me, who is equally fkilled in the art
of growing rich.

E 3 " We

" We laid our money upon camels, concealed in bales of cheap goods, and travelled to the fhore of the red fea. When I caft my eye on the expanfe of waters my heart bounded like that of a prifoner efcaped.   I felt an unextinguifh-able curiofity kindle in my mind, and refolved to fnatch this opportunity of feeing the manners of other nations, and of learning fciences unknown in A-biffinia.

" I remembered that my father had obliged me to the improvement of my ftock, not by a promife which I ought not to violate, but by a penalty which I was at liberty to incur, and therefore de-termined to gratify my predominant defire, and by drinking at the fountains of know-ledge, to quench the thirft of curiofity.

" As

" As I was fuppofed to trade without connexion with my father, it was eafy for me to become acquainted with the mafter of a fhip, and procure a paffage to fome other country. I had no motives of choice to regulate my voyage ; it was fufficient for me that, wherever I wandered, I fhould fee a country which I had not feen before. I therefore entered a fhip bound for Surat, having left a letter for my father declaring my intention.

E 4   CHAP.

C H A P.   IX.

The hiftory of Imlac con-tinued.

WHEN I firft entered upon the world of waters, and loft fight of land, I looked round about me with pleafing terrour, and thinking my foul enlarged by the boundlefs profpect, ima-gined that I could gaze round for ever without fatiety; but, in a fhort time, I grew weary of looking on barren uni-formity, where I could only fee again what I had already feen. I then defcend-ed into the fhip, and doubted for a while whether all my future pleafures would not end like this in difguft and difappoint-ment.

ment. Yet, furely, faid I, the ocean and the land are very different; the only variety of water is reft and motion, but the earth has mountains and vallies, defarts and cities: it is inhabited by men of different cuftoms and contrary opinions; and I may hope to find variety in life, though I fhould mifs it in nature.

" With this hope I quieted my mind, and amufed myfelf during the voyage; fometimes by learning from the failòrs the art of navigation, which I have never practifed, and fometimes by forming fchemes for my conduct in different fituations, in not one of which I have been ever placed.

" I was almoft weary of my naval amufements when we landed fafely at Surat. I

fe-

fecured my money, and purchafing fome
commodities for fhow, joined myfelf to
a caravan that was paffing into the inland country. My companions, for fome
reafon or other, conjecturing that I was
rich, and, by my inquiries and admiration, finding that I was ignorant, confidered me as a novice whom they had a
right to cheat, and who was to learn at
the ufual expence the art of fraud. They
expofed me to the theft of fervants, and
the exaction of officers, and faw me
plundered upon falfe pretences, without
any advantage to themfelves, but that
of rejoicing in the fuperiority of their
own knowledge."

" Stop a moment, faid the prince, is there
fuch depravity in man, as that he fhould
injure another without benefit to himfelf ?

I

I can eafily conceive that all are pleafed with fuperiority ; but your ignorance was merely accidental, which, being neither your crime nor your folly, could afford them no reafon to applaud themfelves; and the knowledge which they had, and which you wanted, they might as effectually have fhewn by warning you, as betraying you."

" Pride, faid Imlac, is feldom delicate, it will pleafe itfelf with very mean advantages ; and envy feels not its own happinefs, but when it may be compared with the mifery of others. They were my enemies becaufe they thought me rich, and my oppreffors becaufe they delighted to find me weak."

" Pro-

" Proceed, faid the prince : I doubt not of the facts which you relate, but imagine that you impute them to miftaken motives."

" In this company, faid Imlac, I arrived at Agra, the capital of Indoftan, the city in which the great Mogul commonly refides. I applied myfelf to the language of the country, and in a few months was able to converfe with the learned men; fome of whom I found morofe and referved, and others eafy and communicative; fome were unwilling to teach another what they had with difficulty learned themfelves; and fome fhewed that the end of their ftudies was to gain the dignity of inftructing.

" To

" To the tutor of the young princes I recommended myfelf fo much, that I was prefented to the emperour as a man of uncommon knowledge. The emperour afked me many queftions concerning my country and my travels; and though I cannot now recollect any thing that he uttered above the power of a common man, he difmiffed me aftonifhed at his wifdom, and enamoured of his goodnefs.

" My credit was now fo high, that the merchants, with whom I had travelled, applied to me for recommendations to the ladies of the court. I was furprifed at their confidence of folicitation, and gently reproached them with their practices on the road. They heard me
with

with cold indifference, and shewed no
tokens of shame or sorrow.

" They then urged their request with
the offer of a bribe; but what I would
not do for kindness I would not do for
money; and refused them, not because
they had injured me, but because I would
not enable them to injure others; for I
knew they would have made use of my
credit to cheat those who should buy their
wares.

" Having resided at Agra, till there
was no more to be learned, I travelled
into Persia, where I saw many remains
of ancient magnificence, and observed
many new accommodations of life. The
Persians are a nation eminently social,
and their assemblies afforded me daily
oppor-

opportunities of remarking characters and manners, and of tracing human nature through all its variations.

" From Perfia I paffed into Arabia, where I faw a nation at once paftoral and warlike; who live without any fettled habitation; whofe only wealth is their flocks and herds; and who have yet carried on, through all ages, an hereditary war with all mankind, though they neither covet nor envy their poffeffions.

C H A P.

C H A P.   X.

Imlac's hiſtory continued.   A diſ-
ſertation upon poetry.

WHEREVER I went, I found
that Poetry was conſidered as the
higheſt learning, and regarded with a ve-
neration ſomewhat approaching to that
which man would pay to the Angelick
Nature.   And it yet fills me with wonder, that, in almoſt all countries, the
moſt ancient poets are conſidered as the
beſt: whether it be that every other
kind of knowledge is an acquiſition
gradually attained, and poetry is a gift
conferred at once; or that the firſt
poetry of every nation ſurpriſed them as

a novelty, and retained the credit by con-
fent which it received by accident at firft :
or whether the province of poetry is to
defcribe Nature and Paffion, which are
always the fame, and the firft writers took
poffeffion of the moft ftriking objects for
defcription, and the moft probable occurrences for fiction, and left nothing to
thofe that followed them, but tranfcrip-
tion of the fame events, and new combinations of the fame images. Whatever
be the reafon, it is commonly obferved that
the early writers are in poffeffion of nature,
and their followers of art : that the firft
excel in ftrength and invention, and the
latter in elegance and refinement.

" I was defirous to add my name to this
illuftrious fraternity. I read all the poets
of Perfia and Arabia, and was able to

repeat by memory the volumes that are
fufpended in the mofque of Mecca. But
1 foon found that no man was ever great
by imitation. My defire of excellence
impelled me to transfer my attention to
nature and to life. Nature was to be
my fubject, and men to be my auditors :
I could never defcribe what I had not
feen : I could not hope to move thofe
with delight or terrour, whofe interefts
and opinions I did not underftand.

" Being now refolved to be a poet, I faw
every thing with a new purpofe; my fphere
of attention was fuddenly magnified : no
kind of knowledge was to be overlooked.
I ranged mountains and deferts for images
and refemblances, and pictured upon my
mind every tree of the foreft and flower
of the valley. I obferved with equal
care

care the crags of the rock and the pinnacles of the palace. Sometimes I wandered along the mazes of the rivulet, and fometimes watched the changes of the fummer clouds. To a poet nothing can be ufelefs. Whatever is beautiful, and whatever is dreadful, muft be familiar to his imagination : he muft be converfant with all that is awfully vaft or elegantly little. The plants of the garden, the animals of the wood, the minerals of the earth, and meteors of the fky, muft all concur to ftore his mind with inexhauftible variety : for every idea is ufeful for the inforcement or decoration of moral or religious truth; and he, who knows moft, will have moft power of diverfifying his fcenes, and of gratifying his reader with remote allufions and unexpected inftruction.

F 2

" All

" All the appearances of nature I was therefore careful to study, and every country which I have surveyed has contributed something to my poetical powers."

" In so wide a survey, said the prince, you must surely have left much unobserved. I have lived, till now, within the circuit of these mountains, and yet cannot walk abroad without the sight of something which I had never beheld before, or never heeded."

" The business of a poet, said Imlac, is to examine, not the individual, but the species; to remark general properties and large appearances : he does not number the streaks of the tulip, or describe the different shades in the ver-

dure

dure of the foreſt. He is to exhibit in his portraits of nature ſuch prominent and ſtriking features, as recal the original to every mind; and muſt neglect the minuter diſcriminations, which one may have remarked, and another have neglected, for thoſe characteriſticks which are alike obvious to vigilance and careleſ-neſs.

" But the knowledge of nature is only half the taſk of a poet; he muſt be acquainted likewiſe with all the modes of life. His character requires that he eſtimate the happineſs and miſery of every condition; obſerve the power of all the paſſions in all their combinations, and trace the changes of the human mind as they are modified by various inſtitutions and accidental influences of climate or cuſtom, from the ſprite-

F 3 lineſs

linefs of infancy to the defpondence of
decrepitude. He muft diveft himfelf of
the prejudices of his age or country; he
muft confider right and wrong in their
abftraƈted and invariable ftate; he muft
difregard prefent laws and opinions,
and rife to general and tranfcendental
truths, which will always be the fame :
he muft therefore content himfelf .with
the flow progrefs of his name; con-
temn the applaufe of his own time,
and commit his claims to the juftice of pof-
terity. He muft write as the interpreter
of nature, and the legiflator of mankind,
and confider himfelf as prefiding over
the thoughts and manners of fucceffive
generations; as a being fuperiour to time
and place. His labour is not yet at an
end : he muft know many languages
and many fciences; and, that his ftile

may

may be worthy of his thoughts, muft, by inceffant practice, familiarize to himfelf every delicacy of fpeech and grace of· harmony."

C H A P. XI.

Imlac's narrative continued. A hint on pilgrimage.

IMLAC now felt the enthufiaftic fit, and was proceeding to aggrandize his own profeffion, when the prince cried out, "Enough! Thou haft convinced me, that no human being can ever be a poet. Proceed now with thy narration."

"To be a poet, faid Imlac, is indeed very difficult." "So difficult, returned the prince, that I will at prefent hear no

more

more of his labours. Tell me whither
you went when you had feen Perfia."

" From Perfia, faid the poet, I travelled through Syria, and for three years
refided in Paleftine, where I converfed
with great numbers of the northern and
weftern nations of Europe; the nations
which are now in poffeffion of all power
and all knowledge; whofe armies are ir-
refiftible, and whofe fleets command the
remoteft parts of the globe. When I
compared thefe men with the natives of
our own kingdom, and thofe that fur-
round us, they appeared almoft another
order of beings. In their countries it is
difficult to wifh for any thing that may
not be obtained: a thoufand arts, of
which we never heard, are continually
labouring for their convenience and pleafure ;

fure; and whatever their own climate has
denied them is fupplied by their commerce."

" By what means, faid the prince, are
the Europeans thus powerful? or why,
fince they can fo eafily vifit Afia and A-
frica for trade or conqueft, cannot the
Afiaticks and Africans invade their coafts,
plant colonies in their ports, and give
laws to their natural princes? The fame
wind that carries them back would bring
us thither."

" They are more powerful, Sir, than
we, anfwered Imlac, becaufe they are
wifer; knowledge will always predominate over ignorance, as man governs the
other animals. But why their knowledge is more than ours, I know not what
rea-

reafon can be given, but the unfearchable will of the Supreme Being."

" When, faid the prince with a figh, fhall I be able to vifit Paleftine, and mingle with this mighty confluence of nations? Till that happy moment fhall arrive, let me fill up the time with fuch reprefentations as thou canft give me. I am not ignorant of the motive that affembles fuch numbers in that place, and cannot but confider it as the center of wifdom and piety, to which the beft and wifeft men of every land muft be continually reforting."

" There are fome nations, faid Imlac, that fend few vifitants to Paleftine; for many numerous and learned fects in Europe, concur to cenfure pilgrimage

as fuperftitious, or deride it as ridicu-
lous."

" You know, faid the prince, how
little my life has made me acquainted
with diverfity of opinions : it will be too
long to hear the arguments on both
fides ; you, that have confidered them,
tell me the refult."

" Pilgrimage, faid Imlac, like many
other acts of piety, may be reafonable
or fuperftitious, according to the princi-
ples upon which it is performed. Long
journies in fearch of truth are not commanded. Truth, fuch as is neceffary to
the regulation of life, is always found
where it is honeftly fought. Change of
place is no natural caufe of the increafe
of piety, for it inevitably produces dif-

fipation

fipation of mind. Yet, fince men go every day to view the places where great actions have been performed, and return with ftronger impreffions of the event, curiofity of the fame kind may naturally difpofe us to view that country whence our religion had its beginning; and I believe no man furveys thofe awful fcenes without fome confirmation of holy refolutions. That the Supreme Being may be more eafily propitiated in one place than in another, is the dream of idle fuperftition; but that fome places may operate upon our own minds in an un-common manner, is an opinion which hourly experience will juftify. He who fuppofes that his vices may be more fuc-cefsfully combated in Paleftine, will, perhaps, find himfelf miftaken, yet he may go thither without folly: he who

who thinks they will be more freely pardoned, dishonours at once his reason and religion."

" These, said the prince, are European distinctions. I will consider them another time. What have you found to be the effect of knowledge? Are those nations happier than we?"

" There is so much infelicity, said the poet, in the world, that scarce any man has leisure from his own distresses to estimate the comparative happiness of others. Knowledge is certainly one of the means of pleasure, as is confessed by the natural desire which every mind feels of increasing its ideas. Ignorance is mere privation, by which nothing can be produced: it is a vacuity in which the soul sits motionless and torpid for want of at-

traction;

traction; and, without knowing why, we always rejoice when we learn, and grieve when we forget. I am therefore inclined to conclude, that, if nothing counteracts the natural confequence of learning, we grow more happy as our minds take a wider range.

" In enumerating the particular comforts of life we fhall find many advantages on the fide of the Europeans. They cure wounds and difeafes with which we languifh and perifh. We fuffer inclemencies of weather which they can obviate. They have engines for the defpatch of many laborious works, which we muft perform by manual induftry. There is fuch communication between diftant places, that one friend can hardly be faid to be abfent from another. Their policy

policy removes all publick inconvenien-
cies : they have roads cut through their
mountains, and bridges laid upon their
rivers.   And, if we defcend to the privacies of life, their habitations are more
commodious, and their poffeffions are
more fecure."

" They are furely happy, faid the
prince, who have all thefe conveniencies, of which I envy none fo much as
the facility with which feparated friends
interchange their thoughts."

" The Europeans, anfwered Imlac,
are lefs unhappy than we, but they are
not happy.   Human life is every where
a ftate in which much is to be endured,
and little to be enjoyed."

CHAP.

C H A P. XII.

The ſtory of Imlac continued.

" I AM not yet willing, ſaid the prince, to ſuppoſe that happineſs is ſo par-ſimoniouſly diſtributed to mortals ; nor can believe but that, if I had the choice of life, I ſhould be able to fill every day with pleaſure. I would injure no man, and ſhould provoke no reſentment: I would relieve every diſtreſs, and ſhould enjoy the benedictions of gratitude. I would chooſe my friends among the wiſe, and my wife among the virtuous ; and therefore ſhould be in no danger from treachery, or unkindneſs. My children ſhould, by my care, be learned and pious,

and

and would repay to my age what their childhood had received. What would dare to moleft him who might call on every fide to thoufands enriched by his bounty, or affifted by his power? And why fhould not life glide quietly away in the foft reciprocation of protection and reverence? All this may be done without the help of European refinements, which appear by their effects to be rather fpecious than ufeful. Let us leave them and perfue our journey."

"From Paleftine, faid Imlac, I paffed through many regions of Afia; in the more civilized kingdoms as a trader, and among the Barbarians of the mountains as a pilgrim. At laft I began to long for my native country, that I might repofe after my travels, and fatigues, in the

VOL. I.   G   places

places where I had fpent my earlieft years, and gladden my old companions with the recital of my adventures. Often did I figure to myfelf thofe, with whom I had fported away the gay hours of dawning life, fitting round me in its evening, wondering at my tales, and liftening to my counfels.

" When this thought had taken pof-feffion of my mind, I confidered every moment as wafted which did not bring me nearer to Abiffinia. I haftened into Egypt, and, notwithftanding my impatience, was detained ten months in the contemplation of its ancient magnificence, and in enquiries after the remains of its ancient learning. I found in Cairo a mixture of all nations ; fome brought thither by the love of knowledge, fome by the hope of gain,

gain, and many by the defire of living after their own manner without obferva-tion, and of lying hid in the obfcurity of multitudes: for, in a city, populous as Cairo, it is poffible to obtain at the fame time the gratifications of fociety, and the fecrecy of folitude.

" From Cairo I travelled to Suez, and embarked on the red fea, paffing a-long the coaft till I arrived at the port from which I had departed twenty years before. Here I joined myfelf to a cara-van and re entered my native country. .

" I now expected the careffes of my kinfmen, and the congratulations of my friends, and was not without hope that my father, whatever value he had fet upon riches, would own with gladnefs

and

and pride a fon who was able to add to the felicity and honour of the nation. But I was foon convinced that my thoughts were vain. My father had been dead fourteen years, having divided his wealth among my brothers, who were removed to fome other provinces. Of my companions the greater part was in the grave, of the reft fome could with difficulty remember me, and fome confidered me as one corrupted by foreign manners.

" A man ufed to viciffitudes is not eafily dejected. I forgot, after a time, my difappointment, and endeavoured to recommend myfelf to the nobles of the kingdom : they admitted me to their tables, heard my ftory, and difmiffed me. I opened a fchool, and was prohibited to teach. I then refolved to fit down in the

quiet

quiet of domeſtick life, and addreſſed a
lady that was fond of my converſation,
but rejeĉted my ſuit, becauſe my father
was a merchant.

" Wearied at laſt with ſolicitation and
repulſes, I reſolved to hide myſelf for
ever from the world, and depend no
longer on the opinion or caprice of others.
I waited for the time when the gate of
the *happy valley* ſhould open, that I might
bid farewell to hope and fear : the day
came; my performance was diſtinguiſhed
with favour, and I reſigned myſelf with
joy to perpetual confinement."

" Haſt thou here found happineſs at
laſt ? ſaid Raſſelas. Tell me without
reſerve; art thou content with thy condition ? or, doſt thou wiſh to be again

wan-

wandering and inquiring? All the inhabitants of this valley celebrate their lot,
and, at the annual vifit of the emperour,
invite others to partake of their felicity."

" Great prince, fajd Imlac, I fhall
fpeak the truth : I know not one of all
your attendants who does not lament the
hour when he entered this retreat. I am
lefs unhappy than the reft, becaufe I have
a mind replete with images, which I can
vary and combine at pleafure. I can
amufe my folitude by the renovation of
the knowledge which begins to fade from
my memory, and with the recollection of
the accidents of my paft life. Yet all
this ends in the forrowful confideration,
that my acquirements are now ufelefs, and
that none of my pleafures can be again
en-

enjoyed. The reft, whofe minds have no impreffion but of the prefent moment, are either corroded by malignant paffions, or fit ftupid in the gloom of perpetual vacancy."

" What paffions can infeft thofe, faid the prince, who have no rivals? We are in a place where impotence precludes malice, and where all envy is repreffed by community of enjoyments."

" There may be community, faid Imlac, of material poffeffions, but there can never be community of love or of efteem. It muft happen that one will pleafe more than another; he that knows himfelf defpifed will always be envious; and ftill more envious and malevolent, if he is condemned to live in the prefence of thofe who defpife him. The invitations, by which they allure others to a ftate which they feel to be wretched, proceed from the natural malignity of hopelefs mifery. They are weary of themfelves, and of each other, and expect to find relief in new companions. They envy the liberty which their folly has forfeited, and would gladly fee all mankind imprifoned like themfelves.

" From this crime, however, I am wholly free. No man can fay that he is wretched by my perfuafion. I look with pity on the crowds who are annually foliciting admiffion to captivity, and wifh that it were lawful for me to warn them of their danger."

" My

" My dear Imlac, faid the prince, I will open to thee my whole heart, that I have long meditated an efcape from the happy valley. I have examined the mountains on every fide, but find myfelf infuperably barred : teach me the way to break my prifon ; thou fhalt be the companion of my flight, the guide of my rambles, the partner of my fortune, and my fole director in the *choice of life*."

" Sir, anfwered the poet, your efcape will be difficult, and, perhaps, you may foon repent your curiofity. The world, which you figure to yourfelf fmooth and quiet as the lake in the valley, you will find a fea foaming with tempefts, and boiling with whirlpools : you will be fometimes overwhelmed by the waves of

vio-

violence, and fometimes dafhed againft the rocks of treachery. Amidft wrongs and frauds, competitions and anxieties, you will wifh a thoufand times for thefe feats of quiet, and willingly quit hope to be free from fear."

" Do not feek to deter me from my purpofe, faid the prince : I am impatient to fee what thou haft feen; and, fince thou art thyfelf weary of the valley, it is evident, that thy former ftate was better than this. Whatever be the confequence of my experiment, I am refolved to judge with my own eyes of the various conditions of men, and then to make deliberately my *choice of life*."

" I am afraid, faid Imlac, you are hindered by ftronger reftraints than my per-

perfuafions; yet, if your determination is fixed, I do not counfel you to defpair. Few things are impoffible to diligence and fkill."

C H A P. XIII.

Raffelas difcovers the means of efcape.

THE prince now difmiffed his favourite to reft, but the narrative of wonders and novelties filled his mind with perturbation. He revolved all that he had heard, and prepared innumerable queftions for the morning.

Much of his uneafinefs was now removed. He had a friend to whom he could

could impart his thoughts, and whofe experience could affift him in his defigns. His heart was no longer condemned to fwell with filent vexation. He thought that even the *happy valley* might be endured with fuch a companion, and that, if they could range the world together, he fhould have nothing further to defire.

In a few days the water was difcharged, and the ground dried. The prince and Imlac then walked out together to con-verfe without the notice of the reft. The prince, whofe thoughts were always on the wing, as he paffed by the gate, faid, with a countenance of forrow, " Why art thou fo ftrong, and why is man fo weak ?"

" Man

" Man is not weak, anfwered his companion; knowledge is more than equivalent to force. The mafter of mecha-
nicks laughs at ftrength. I can burft the
gate, but cannot do it fecretly. Some
other expedient muft be tried."

As they were walking on the fide of
the mountain, they obferved that the
conies, which the rain had driven from
their burrows, had taken fhelter among
the bufhes, and formed holes behind
them, tending upwards in an oblique
line. " It has been the opinion of antiquity, faid Imlac, that human reafon
borrowed many arts from the inftinct
of animals; let us, therefore, not think
ourfelves degraded by learning from the
coney. We may efcape by piercing the
mountain in the fame direction. We
will

will begin where the fummit hangs over the middle part, and labour upward till we fhall iffue out beyond the prominence."

The eyes of the prince, when he heard this propofal, fparkled with joy. The execution was eafy, and the fuccefs certain.

No time was now loft. They haftened early in the morning to chufe a place proper for their mine. They clambered with great fatigue among crags and brambles, and returned without having difcovered any part that favoured their defign. The fecond and the third day were fpent in the fame manner, and with the fame fruftration. But, on the fourth, they found a fmall cavern, con-

cealed

cealed by a thicket, where they refolved to make their experiment.

Imlac procured inftruments proper to hew ftone and remove earth, and they fell to their work on the next day with more eagernefs than vigour. They were prefently exhaufted by their efforts, and fat down to pant upon the grafs. The prince, for a moment, appeared to be difcouraged. " Sir, faid his companion, practice will enable us to continue our labour for a longer time ; mark, however, how far we have advanced, and you will find that our toil will fome time have an end. Great works are performed, not by ftrength, but perfeverance : yonder palace was raifed by fingle ftones, yet you fee its height and fpacioufnefs. He that fhall walk with vigour three hours a day will

will pafs in feven years a fpace equal to the circumference of the globe."

They returned to their labour day after day, and, in a fhort time, found a fiffure in the rock, which enabled them to pafs far with very little obftruction. This Raffelas confidered as a good omen. " Do not difturb your mind, faid Imlac, with other hopes or fears than reafon may fuggeft: if you are pleafed with prognofticks of good, you will be terrified likewife with tokens of evil, and your whole life will be a prey to fuperftition. Whatever facilitates our work is more than an omen, it is a caufe of fuccefs. This is one of thofe pleafing furprifes which often happen to active refolution. Many things difficult to defign prove eafy to performance."

CHAP.

CHAP. XIV.

Raffelas and Imlac receive an un-expected vifit.

THEY had now wrought their way to the middle, and folaced their labour with the approach of liberty, when the prince, coming down to refrefh himfelf with air, found his fifter Nekayah ftanding before the mouth of the cavity. He ftarted and ftood confufed, afraid to tell his defign, and yet hopelefs to conceal it. A few moments determined him to repofe on her fidelity, and fecure her fecrecy by a declaration without referve.

" Do not imagine, faid the princefs, that I came hither as a fpy: I had often obferved from my window, that you and

Imlac directed your walk every day towards the fame point, but I did not fuppofe you had any better reafon for the
preference than a cooler fhade, or more
fragrant bank ; nor followed you with
any other defign than to partake of your
converfation. Since then not fufpicion
but fondnefs has detected you, let me
not lofe the advantage of my difcovery.
I am equally weary of confinement with
yourfelf, and not lefs defirous of knowing what is done or fuffered in the world.
Permit me to fly with you from this
taftelefs tranquility, which will yet grow
more loathfome when you have left me.
You may deny me to accompany you,
but cannot hinder me from following."

The prince, who loved Nekayah above
his other fifters, had no inclination to
refufe

refuſe her requeſt, and grieved that he had loſt an opportunity of ſhewing his confidence by a voluntary communication. It was therefore agreed that ſhe ſhould leave the valley with them ; and that, in the mean time, ſhe ſhould watch, left any other ſtraggler ſhould, by chance or curioſity, follow them to the mountain.

At length their labour was at an end ; they ſaw light beyond the prominence, and, iſſuing to the top of the mountain, beheld the Nile, yet a narrow current, wandering beneath them.

The prince looked round with rapture, anticipated all the pleaſures of travel, and in thought was already tranſported beyond his father's dominions. Imlac,

H 2   though

though very joyful at his efcape, had lefs expectation of pleafure in the world, which he had before tried, and of which he had been weary.

Raffelas was fo much delighted with a wider horizon, that he could not foon be perfuaded to return into the valley. He informed his fifter that the way was open, and that nothing now remained but to prepare for their departure.

CHAP.

C H A P.   XV.

The prince and princefs leave the valley, and fee many wonders.

T H E prince and princefs had jewels fufficient to make them rich when-ever they came into a place of commerce, which, by Imlac's direction, they hid in their cloaths, and, on the night of the next full moon, all left the valley. The princefs was followed only by a fingle fa-vourite, who did not know whither fhe was going.

They clambered through the cavity, and began to go down on the other fide. The princefs and her maid turned their

H 3   eyes

eyes towards every part, and, feeing nothing to bound their profpect, confidered
themfelves as in danger of being loft in
a dreary vacuity. They ftopped and
trembled. "I am almoft afraid, faid the
princefs, to begin a journey of which I
cannot perceive an end, and to venture
into this immenfe plain where I may be
approached on every fide by men whom
I never faw." The prince felt nearly the
fame emotions, though he thought it
more manly to conceal them.

Imlac fmiled at their terrours, and
encouraged them to proceed; but the
princefs continued irrefolute till fhe had
been imperceptibly drawn forward too
far to return.

In

In the morning they found some shep-
herds in the field, who set milk and fruits
before them. The princess wondered
that she did not see a palace ready for her
reception, and a table spread with delicacies; but, being faint and hungry,
she drank the milk and eat the fruits,
and thought them of a higher flavour
than the products of the valley.

They travelled forward by easy jour-
neys, being all unaccustomed to toil or
difficulty, and knowing, that though
they might be missed, they could not
be pursued.   In a few days they came into a more populous region, where Imlac
was diverted with the admiration which
his companions expressed at the diversity
of manners, stations and employments.

Their

Their drefs was fuch as might not bring
upon them the fufpicion of having any
thing to conceal, yet the prince, where-
ever he came, expected to be obeyed,
and the princefs was frighted, becaufe
thofe that came into her prefence did not
proftrate themfelves before her. Imlac
was forced to obferve them with great
vigilance, left they fhould betray their
rank by their unufual behaviour, and
detained them feveral weeks in the firft
village to accuftom them to the fight of
common mortals.

By degrees the royal wanderers were
taught to underftand that they had for a
time laid afide their dignity, and were to expect only fuch regard as liberality and courtefy could procure. And Imlac, having,
by many admonitions, prepared them to

en-

endure the tumults of a port, and the ruggednefs of the commercial race, brought them down to the fea-coaft.

The prince and his fifter, to whom every thing was new, were gratified equally at all places, and therefore remained for fome months at the port without any inclination to pafs further. Imlac was content with their ftay, becaufe he did not think it fafe to expofe them, unpractifed in the world, to the hazards of a foreign country.

At laft he began to fear left they fhould be difcovered, and propofed to fix a day for their departure. They had no pretenfions to judge for themfelves, and referred the whole fcheme to his direction. He therefore took paffage in a fhip to Suez ;

Suez; and, when the time came, with great difficulty prevailed on the princefs to enter the veffel. They had a quick and profperous voyage, and from Suez travelled by land to Cairo.

C H A P. XVI.

They enter Cairo, and find every man happy.

A S they approached the city, which filled the ftrangers with aftonifh-ment, " This, faid Imlac to the prince, is the place where travellers and mer-chants affemble from all the corners of the earth. You will here find men of every character, and every occupation. Commerce is here honourable : I will act

as

as a merchant, and you shall live as strangers, who have no other end of travel than curiosity; it will soon be observed that we are rich; our reputation will procure us access to all whom we shall desire to know; you will see all the conditions of humanity, and enable yourself at leisure to make your *choice of life.*"

They now entered the town, stunned by the noise, and offended by the crowds. Instruction had not yet so prevailed over habit, but that they wondered to see themselves pass undistinguished along the street, and met by the lowest of the people without reverence or notice. The princess could not at first bear the thought of being levelled with the vulgar, and, for some days, continued in

her

her chamber, where fhe was ferved by her favourite as in the palace of the valley.

Imlac, who underftood traffick, fold part of the jewels the next day, and hired a houfe, which he adorned with fuch magnificence, that he was immediately con-fidered as a merchant of great wealth. His politenefs attracted many acquaintance, and his generofity made him courted by many dependants. His table was crowded by men of every nation, who all admired his knowledge, and folicited his favour. His companions, not being able to mix in the converfation, could make no difcovery of their ignorance or furprife, and were gradually initiated in the world as they gained knowledge of the language.

The

The prince had, by frequent lectures, been taught the use and nature of money; but the ladies could not, for a long time, comprehend what the merchants did with small pieces of gold and silver, or why things of so little use should be received as equivalent to the necessaries of life.

They studied the language two years, while Imlac was preparing to set before them the various ranks and conditions of mankind. He grew acquainted with all who had any thing uncommon in their fortune or conduct. He frequented the voluptuous and the frugal, the idle and the busy, the merchants and the men of learning.

The prince, being now able to converse with fluency, and having learned

the

the caution neceſſary to be obſerved in his intercourſe with ſtrangers, began to accompany Imlac to places of reſort, and to enter into all aſſemblies, that he might make his *choice of life.*

For ſome time he thought choice need-leſs, becauſe all appeared to him equally happy. Wherever he went he met gay-ety and kindneſs, and heard the ſong of joy, or the laugh of carelefneſs. He began to believe that the world over-flowed with univerſal plenty, and that nothing was withheld either from want or merit; that every hand ſhowered li-berality, and every heart melted with be-nevolence : " and who then, ſays he, will be ſuffered to be wretched ? "

Imlac

Imlac permitted the pleasing delusion, and was unwilling to crush the hope of inexperience, till one day, having sat a while silent, " I know not, said the prince, what can be the reason that I am more unhappy than any of our friends. I see them perpetually and unalterably chearful, but feel my own mind restless and uneasy. I am unsatisfied with those pleasures which I seem most to court; I live in the crowds of jollity, not so much to enjoy company as to shun myself, and am only loud and merry to conceal my sadness."

" Every man, said Imlac, may, by examining his own mind, guess what passes in the minds of others: when you feel that your own gaiety is counterfeit, it may justly lead you to suspect that of your

com-

companions not to be fincere. Envy is commonly reciprocal. We are long before we
are convinced that happinefs is never to be
found, and each believes it poffeffed by o-
thers, to keep alive the hope of obtaining
it for himfelf. In the affembly, where you
paffed the laft night, there appeared fuch
fpritelinefs of air, and volatility of fancy,
as might have fuited beings of an higher
order, formed to inhabit ferener regions
inacceffible to care or forrow: yet, believe me, prince, there was not one who
did not dread the moment when folitude
fhould deliver him to the tyranny of
reflection."

" This, faid the prince, may be true
of others, fince it is true of me; yet,
whatever be the general infelicity of man,
one condition is more happy than another,

ther, and wisdom surely directs us to take the least evil in the *choice of life*."

" The causes of good and evil, answered Imlac, are so various and uncertain, so often entangled with each other, so diversified by various relations, and so much subject to accidents which cannot be foreseen, that he who would fix his condition upon incontestable reasons of preference, must live and die enquiring and deliberating."

" But surely, said Rasselas, the wise men, to whom we listen with reverence and wonder, chose that mode of life for themselves which they thought most likely to make them happy."

" Very

" Very few, faid the poet, live by choice. Every man is placed in his prefent condition by caufes which acted without his forefight, and with which he did not always willingly co-operate; and therefore you will rarely meet one who does not think the lot of his neighbour better than his own."

" I am pleafed to think, faid the prince, that my birth has given me at leaft one advantage over others, by enabling me to determine for myfelf. I have here the world before me ; I will review it at leifure : furely happinefs is fomewhere to be found."

CHAP.

C H A P. XVII.

The prince affociates with young
men of fpirit and gaiety.

RASSELAS rofe next day, and refolved to begin his experiments upon
life. "Youth, cried he, is the time of
gladnefs : I will join myfelf to the young
men, whofe only bufinefs is to gratify
their defires, and whofe time is all fpent
in a fucceffion of enjoyments."

To fuch focieties he was readily admitted, but a few days brought him
back weary and difgufted. Their mirth
was without images, their laughter with-

out motive; their pleafures were grofs
and fenfual, in which the mind had no
part; their conduct was at once wild and
mean; they laughed at order and at law,
but the frown of power dejected, and the
eye of wifdom abafhed them.

The prince foon concluded, that he
fhould never be happy in a courfe of life
of which he was afhamed.   He thought
it unfuitable to a reafonable being to act
without a plan, and to be fad or chearful only by chance.   " Happinefs, faid
he, muft be fomething folid and perma-
nent, without fear and without uncer-
tainty."

But his young companions had gained
fo much of his regard by their franknefs
and courtefy, that he could not leave them
with-

without warning and remonftrance. "My friends, faid he, I have ferioufly confidered our manners and our profpeets, and find that we have miftaken our own intereft. The firft years of man muft make provifion for the laft. He that never thinks never can be wife. Perpetual levity muft end in ignorance; and intemperance, though it may fire the fpirits for an hour, will make life fhort or miferable. Let us confider that youth is of no long duration, and that in maturer age, when the enchantments of fancy fhall ceafe, and phantoms of delight dance no more about us, we fhall have no comforts but the efteem of wife men, and the means of doing good. Let us, therefore, ftop, while to ftop is in our power: let us live as men who are fometime to grow old, and to whom it will

be

be the moſt dreadful of all evils not
to count their paſt years but by follies,
and to be reminded of their former luxuri-
ance of health only by the maladies which
riot has produced."

They ſtared a while in ſilence one upon
another, and, at laſt, drove him away by
a general chorus of continued laughter.

The conſcioufneſs that his ſentiments
were juſt, and his intentions kind, was
ſcarcely fufficient to fupport him againſt
the horrour of deriſion. But he reco-
vered his tranquility, and perſued his
ſearch.

C H A P.

C H A P. XVIII.

The prince finds a wife and happy man.

A S he was one day walking in the ftreet, he faw a fpacious building which all were, by the open doors, invited to enter: he followed the ftream of people, and found it a hall or fchool of declamation, in which profeffors read lectures to their auditory. He fixed his eye upon a fage raifed above the reft, who difcourfed with great energy on the government of the paffions. His look was venerable, his action graceful, his pronunciation clear, and his diction elegant. He fhewed, with great ftrength of fentiment,

I 4   and

and variety of illuftration, that human
nature is degraded and debafed, when
the lower faculties predominate over the
higher; that when fancy, the parent of
paffion, ufurps the dominion of the mind,
nothing enfues but the natural effect of
unlawful government, perturbation and
confufion; that fhe betrays the fortreffes of
the intellect to rebels, and excites her
children to fedition againft reafon their
lawful fovereign.   He compared reafon
to the fun, of which the light is conftant, uniform, and lafting; and fancy
to a meteor, of bright but tranfitory
luftre, irregular in its motion, and delufive in its direction.

He then communicated the various
precepts given from time to time for the
conqueft of paffion, and difplayed the
hap-

happinefs of thofe who had obtained the important victory, after which man is no longer the flave of fear, nor the fool of hope; is no more emaciated by envy, inflamed by anger, emafculated by tendernefs, or depreffed by grief; but walks on calmly through the tumults or the privacies of life, as the fun perfues alike his courfe through the calm or the ftormy fky.

He enumerated many examples of heroes immovable by pain or pleafure, who looked with indifference on thofe modes or accidents to which the vulgar give the names of good and evil. He exhorted his hearers to lay afide their prejudices, and arm themfelves againft the fhafts of malice or misfortune, by invulnerab!e patienc ; concluding, that this

this ſtate only was happineſs, and that
this happineſs was in every one's power.

Raſſelas liſtened to him with the vene-
ration due to the inſtructions of a ſuperi-
our being, and, waiting for him at the
door, humbly implored the liberty of
viſiting ſo great a maſter of true wiſdom.
The lecturer heſitated a moment, when
Raſſelas put a purſe of gold into his hand,
which he received with a mixture of joy
and wonder.

" I have found, ſaid the prince, at his
return to Imlac, a man who can teach
all that is neceſſary to be known, who,
from the unſhaken throne of rational for-
titude, looks down on the ſcenes of life
changing beneath him. He ſpeaks, and
attention watches his lips. He reaſons,
and

and conviction clofes his periods. This man fhall be my future guide: I will learn his doctrines, and imitate his life.",

" Be not too hafty, faid Imlac, to truft, or to admire, the teachers of morality: they difcourfe like angels, but they live like men."

Raffelas, who could not conceive how any man could reafon fo forcibly without feeling the cogency of his own arguments, paid his vifit in a few days, and was denied admiffion. He had now learned the power of money, and made his way by a piece of gold to the inner apartment, where he found the philofopher in a room half darkened, with his eyes mifty, and his face pale. " Sir, faid he, you are come at a time when all human friend-

fhip

ſhip is uſeleſs ; what I ſuffer cannot be remedied, what I have loſt cannot be ſupplied. My daughter, my only daughter, from whoſe tenderneſs I expected all the comforts of my age, died laſt night of a fever. My views, my purpoſes, my hopes are at an end : I am now a lonely being diſunited from ſociety."

" Sir, ſaid the prince, mortality is an event by which a wiſe man can never be ſurpriſed : we know that death is always near, and it ſhould therefore always be expected." " Young man, anſwered the philoſopher, you ſpeak like one that has never felt the pangs of ſeparation." " Have you then forgot the precepts, ſaid Raſſelas, which you ſo powerfully enforced ? Has wiſdom no ſtrength to arm the heart againſt calamity ? Conſider, that

that external things are naturally vari-
able, but truth and reafon are always the
fame." "What comfort, faid the mourn-
er, can truth and reafon afford me? of
what effect are they now, but to tell me,
that my daughter will not be reftored?"

The prince, whofe humanity would
not fuffer him to infult mifery with re-
proof, went away convinced of the emp-
tinefs of rhetorical found, and the inef-
ficacy of polifhed periods and ftudied fen-
tences.

CHAP.

C H A P. XIX.

A Glimpfe of paftoral life.

HE was ftill eager upon the fame enquiry; and, having heard of a
hermit, that lived near the loweft cataract of the Nile, and filled the whole
country with the fame of his fanctity,
refolved to vifit his retreat, and enquire
whether that felicity, which publick life
could not afford, was to be found in folitude ; and whether a man, whofe age
and virtue made him venerable, could
teach any peculiar art of fhunning evils,
or enduring them.

Imlac

Imlac and the princefs agreed to accompany him, and, after the neceffary
preparations, they began their journey.
Their way lay through fields, where
fhepherds tended their flocks, and the
lambs were playing upon the pafture.
" This, faid the poet, is the life which
has been often celebrated for its innocence
and quiet: let us pafs the heat of the
day among the fhepherds tents, and know
whether all our fearches are not to termi-
nate in paftoral fimplicity."

The propofal pleafed them, and they
induced the fhepherds, by fmall prefents
and familiar queftions, to tell their opinion of their own ftate: they were fo
rude and ignorant, fo little able to compare the good with the evil of the
occupation, and fo indiftinct in their nar-

I ratives

ratives and defcriptions, that very little could be learned from them. But it was evident that their hearts were cankered with difcontent; that they confidered themfelves as condemned to labour for the luxury of the rich, and look-ed up with ftupid malevolence toward thofe that were placed above them.

The princefs pronounced with vehe-mence, that fhe would never fuffer thefe envious favages to be her companions, and that fhe fhould not foon be defirous of feeing any more fpecimens of ruftick happinefs; but could not believe that all the accounts of primeval pleafures were fabulous, and was yet in doubt whether life had any thing that could be juftly preferred to the placid gratifications of fields and woods. She hoped that the

time

time would come, when, with a few virtuous and elegant companions, fhe fhould
gather flowers planted by her own hand,
fondle the lambs of her own ewe, and
liften, without care, among brooks and
breezes, to one of her maidens reading
in the fhade.

C H A P. XX.

The danger of profperity.

ON the next day they continued their
journey, till the heat compelled
them to look round for fhelter. At a
fmall diftance they faw a thick wood,
which they no fooner entered than they
perceived that they were approaching the
habitations of men. The fhrubs were

diligently cut away to open walks where the fhades were darkeft; the boughs of oppofite trees were artificially interwoven; feats of flowery turf were raifed in vacant fpaces, and a rivulet, that wantoned along the fide of a winding path, had its banks fometimes opened into fmall bafons, and its ftream fometimes obftruĉted by little mounds of ftone heaped together to increafe its mur-murs.

They paffed flowly through the wood, delighted with fuch unexpeĉted accommodations, and entertained each other with conjeĉturing what, or who, he could be, that, in thofe rude and unfrequented regions, had leifure and art for fuch harmlefs luxury.

As

As they advanced, they heard the found of mufick, and faw youths and virgins dancing in the grove; and, going ftill further, beheld a ftately palace built upon a hill furrounded with woods. The laws of eaftern hofpitality allowed them to enter, and the mafter welcomed them like a man liberal and wealthy.

He was fkilful enough in appearances foon to difcern that they were no common guefts, and fpread his table with magnificence. The eloquence of Imlac caught his attention, and the lofty courtefy of the princefs excited his refpect. When they offered to depart he entreated their ftay, and was the next day ftill more unwilling to difmifs them than before. They were eafily perfuaded to

ftop,

ftop, and civility grew up in time to freedom and confidence.

The prince now faw all the domefticks chearful, and all the face of nature fmiling round the place, and could not forbear to hope that he fhould find here what he was feeking ; but when he was congratulating the mafter upon his poffeffions, he anfwered with a figh, " My condition has indeed the appearance of happinefs, but appearances are delufive. My profperity puts my life in danger ; the Baffa of Egypt is my enemy, incenfed only by my wealth and popularity. I have been hitherto protected againft him by the princes of the country ; but, as the favour of the great is uncertain, I know not how foon my defenders may be perfuaded to fhare the plunder with

the

the Baſſa. I have ſent my treaſures into a diſtant country, and, upon the firſt alarm, am prepared to follow them. Then will my enemies riot in my manſion, and enjoy the gardens which I have planted.''

They all joined in lamenting his danger, and deprecating his exile; and the princeſs was ſo much diſturbed with the tumult of grief and indignation, that ſhe retired to her apartment. They continued with their kind inviter a few days longer, and then went forward to find the hermit.

CHAP.

C H A P.   XXI.

The happinefs of folitude.   The hermit's hiftory.

THEY came on the third day, by the direction of the peafants, to the hermit's cell: it was a cavern in the fide of a mountain, over-fhadowed with palm-trees ; at fuch a diftance from the cataract, that nothing more was heard than a gentle uniform murmur, fuch as compofed the mind to penfive meditation, efpecially when it was affift-ed by the wind whiftling among the branches.   The firft rude effay of nature had been fo much improved by human labour, that the cave contained feveral

apart-

apartments, appropriated to different ufes, and often afforded lodging to travellers, whom darknefs or tempefts happened to overtake.

The hermit fat on a bench at the door, to enjoy the coolnefs of the evening. On one fide lay a book with pens and papers, on the other mechanical inftruments of various kinds. As they approached him unregarded, the princefs obferved that he had not the countenance of a man that had found, or could teach, the way to happinefs.

They faluted him with great refpect, which he repaid like a man not unaccuftomed to the forms of courts. " My children, faid he, if you have loft your way, you fhall be willingly fupplied with

K 4   fuch

fuch conveniencies for the night as th's cavern will afford. I have all that nature requires, and you will not expect delicacies in a hermit's cell."

They thanked him, and, entering, were pleafed with the neatnefs and regularity of the place. The hermit fet flefh and wine before them, though he fed only upon fruits and water. His difcourfe was chearful without levity, and pious without enthufiafm. He foon gained the efteem of his guefts, and the princefs repented of her hafty cenfure.

At laft Imlac began thus: " I do not now wonder that your reputation is fo far extended ; we have heard at Cairo of your wifdom, and came hither to implore

plore your direction for this young man and maiden in the *choice of life.*"

" To him that lives well, anfwered the hermit, every form of life is good; nor can I give any other rule for choice, than to remove from all apparent evil."

" He will remove moft certainly from evil, faid the prince, who fhall devote himfelf to that folitude which you have recommended by your example."

" I have indeed lived fifteen years in folitude, faid the hermit, but have no defire that my example fhould gain any imitators. In my youth I profeffed arms, and was raifed by degrees to the higheft military rank. I have traverfed wide countries at the head of my troops, and

feen

feen many battles and fieges. At laft, being difgufted by the preferment of a younger officer, and finding my vigour beginning to decay, I refolved to clofe my life in peace, having found the world full of fnares, difcord, and mifery. I had once efcaped from the perfuit of the enemy by the fhelter of this cavern, and therefore chofe it for my final refidence. I employed artificers to form it into chambers, and ftored it with all that I was likely to want.

" For fome time after my retreat, I rejoiced like a tempeft-beaten failor at his entrance into the harbour, being delighted with the fudden change of the noife and hurry of war, to ftillnefs and repofe. When the pleafure of novelty went away, I employed my hours in examining

amining the plants which grow in the valley, and the minerals which I collected from the rocks. But that enquiry is now grown taftelefs and irkfome. I have been for fome time unfettled and diftracted : my mind is difturbed with a thoufand perplexities of doubt, and vanities of imagination, which hourly prevail upon me, becaufe I have no opportunities of relaxation or diverfion. I am fometimes afhamed to think that I could not fecure myfelf from vice, but by retiring from the practice of virtue, and begin to fufpect that I was rather impelled by refentment, than led by devotion, into folitude. My fancy riots in fcenes of folly, and I lament that I have loft fo much, and have gained fo little. In folitude, if I efcape the example of bad men, I want likewife the

con-

counfel and converfation of the good.
I have been long comparing the evils
with the advantages of fociety, and re-
folve to return into the world to morrow.
The life of a folitary man will be certainly miferable, but not certainly devout."

They heard his refolution with furprife, but, after a fhort paufe, offered
to conduct him to Cairo. He dug up a
confiderable treafure which he had hid
among the rocks, and accompanied them
to the city, on which, as he approached
it, he gazed with rapture.

CHAP.

C H A P. XXII.

The happinefs of a life led according to nature.

RASSSELAS went often to an affembly of learned men, who met at ftated times to unbend their minds, and compare their opinions. Their manners were fomewhat coarfe, but their converfation was inftructive, and their difputations acute, though fometimes too violent, and often continued till neither controvertift remembered upon what queftion they began. Some faults were almoft general among them : every one was defirous to dictate to the reft, and every one was pleafed to

hear

hear the genius or knowledge of another depreciated.

In this affembly Raffelas was relating his interview with the hermit, and the wonder with which he heard him cenfure a courfe of life which he had fo deliberately chofen, and fo laudably followed. The fentiments of the hearers were various. Some were of opinion, that the folly of his choice had been juftly punifhed by condemnation to perpetual perfeverance. One of the youngeft among them, with great vehemence, pronounced him an hypocrite. Some talked of the right of fociety to the labour of individuals, and confidered retirement as a defertion of duty. Others readily allowed, that there was a time when the claims of the publick were fatisfied,

tisfied, and when a man might properly fequefter himfelf, to review his life, and purify his heart.

One, who appeared more affected with the narrative than the reft, thought it likely, that the hermit would, in a few years, go back to his retreat, and, perhaps, if fhame did not reftrain, or death intercept him, return once more from his retreat into the world: " For the hope of happinefs, fays he, is fo ftrongly impreffed, that the longeft experience is not able to efface it. Of the prefent ftate, whatever it be, we feel, and are forced to confefs, the mifery, yet, when the fame ftate is again at a dif-tance, imagination paints it as defirable. But the time will furely come, when de-fire will be no longer our torment, and no man

man fhall be wretched but by his own fault."

" This, faid a philofopher, who had heard him with tokens of great impatience, is the prefent condition of a wife man. The time is already come, when none are wretched but by their own fault. Nothing is more idle, than to enquire after happinefs, which nature has kindly placed within our reach. The way to be happy is to live according to nature, in obedience to that univerfal and unalterable law with which every heart is originally impreffed; which is not written on it by precept, but engraven by deftiny, not inftilled by education, but infufed at our nativity. He that lives according to nature will fuffer nothing from the delufions of hope, or importunities of defire :

fire : he will receive and reject with equa-
bility of temper; and act or suffer as the
reason of things shall alternately pre-
scribe. Other men may amuse themselves with subtle definitions, or intricate
raciocination. Let them learn to be wise
by easier means : let them observe the
hind of the foreft, and the linnet of the
grove : let them confider the life of animals, whofe motions are regulated by
inftinct ; they obey their guide and are
happy. Let us therefore, at length,
ceafe to difpute, and learn to live; throw
away the incumbrance of precepts, which
they who utter them with fo much pride
and pomp do not underftand, and carry
with us this fimple and intelligible max-
im, That deviation from nature is deviation from happinefs."

When he had spoken, he looked round him with a placid air, and enjoyed the confcioufnefs of his own beneficence. "Sir, faid the prince, with great modefty, as I, like all the reft of mankind, am defirous of felicity, my clofeft attention has been fixed upon your difcourfe : I doubt not the truth of a pofition which a man fo learned has fo confidently advanced. Let me only know what it is to live according to nature."

"When I find young men fo humble and fo docile, faid the philofopher, I can deny them no information which my ftudies have enabled me to afford. To live according to nature, is to act always with due regard to the fitnefs arifing from the relations and qualities of caufes and effects; to concur with the great and un-
changeable

changeable fcheme of univerfal felicity; to co-operate with the general difpofi- tion and tendency of the prefent fyftem of things."

The prince foon found that this was one of the fages whom he fhould under- ftand lefs as he heard him longer. He therefore bowed and was filent, and the philofopher, fuppofing him fatisfied, and the reft vanquifhed, rofe up and departed with the air of a man that had co-ope- rated with the prefent fyftem.

L 2   CHAP.

C H A P. XXIII.

The prince and his fifter divide between them the work of obfervation.

RASSELAS returned home full of reflexions, doubtful how to direct his future fteps. Of the way to happinefs he found the learned and fimple equally ignorant; but, as he was yet young, he flattered himfelf that he had time remaining for more experiments, and further enquiries. He communicated to Imlac his obfervations and his doubts, but was anfwered by him with new doubts, and remarks that gave

him

him no comfort. He therefore difcourfed more frequently and freely with his
fifter, who had yet the fame hope with
himfelf, and always affifted him to give
fome reafon why, though he had been
hitherto fruftrated, he might fucceed at
laft.

"We have hitherto, faid fhe, known
but little of the world : we have never yet
been either great or mean. In our own
country, though we had royalty, we had
no power, and in this we have not yet
feen the private receffes of domeftick
peace. Imlac favours not our fearch,
left we fhould in time find him miftaken. We will divide the tafk between
us : you fhall try what is to be found in
the fplendour of courts, and I will range
the fhades of humbler life. Perhaps

com-

command and authority may be the fupreme bleffings, as they afford moft opportunities of doing good : or, perhaps,
what this world can give may be found
in the modeft habitations of middle fortune; too low for great defigns, and too
high for penury and diftrefs."

C H A P.   XXIV.

The prince examines the happinefs of high ftations.

R ASSELAS applauded the defign,
and appeared next day with a
fplendid retinue at the court of the Baffa.
He was foon diftinguifhed for his magnificence, and admitted, as a prince whofe
curiofity had brought him from diftant

countries, to an intimacy with the great officers, and frequent conversation with the Baffa himfelf.

He was at firft inclined to believe, that the man muft be pleafed with his own condition, whom all approached with reverence, and heard with obedience, and who had the power to extend his edicts to a whole kingdom. " There can be no pleafure, faid he, equal to that of feeling at once the joy of thoufands all made happy by wife adminiftration. Yet, fince, by the law of fubordination, this fublime delight can be in one nation but the lot of one, it is furely reafonable to think there is fome fatisfaction more popular and acceffible, and that millions can hardly be fubjected to the will of a fingle

L 4

man,

man, only to fill his particular breaſt
with incommunicable content."

Theſe thoughts were often in his
mind, and he found no ſolution of the
difficulty. But as preſents and civilities
gained him more familiarity, he found
that almoſt every man that ſtood high in
employment hated all the reſt, and was
hated by them, and that their lives were
a continual ſucceſſion of plots and de-
tections, ſtratagems and eſcapes, fac-
tion and treachery. Many of thoſe,
who ſurrounded the Baſſa, were ſent only to watch and report his conduct ; every
tongue was muttering cenſure, and
every eye was ſearching for a fault.

At laſt the letters of revocation arrived, the Baſſa was carried in chains to
Con-

Conftantinople, and his name was men-
tioned no more.

" What are we now to think of the
prerogatives of power, faid Raffelas to
his fifter; is it without any efficacy to
good? or, is the fubordinate degree
only dangerous, and the fupreme fafe
and. glorious? Is the Sultan the only
happy man in his dominions? or, is the
Sultan himfelf fubject to the torments of
fufpicion, and the dread of enemies?"

In a fhort time the fecond Baffa was
depofed. The Sultan, that had advanced
him, was murdered by the Janifaries,
and his fucceffor had other views and
different favourites.

CHAP. XXV.

The princefs perfues her enquiry with more diligence than fuccefs.

THE princefs, in the mean time, infinuated herfelf into many families; for there are few doors, through which liberality, joined with good humour, cannot find its way. The daughters of many houfes were airy and chearful, but Nekayah had been too long accuftomed to the converfation of Imlac and her brother to be much pleafed with childifh levity and prattle which had no meaning. She found their thoughts narrow, their wifhes low, and their merriment

ment often artificial. Their pleasures, poor as they were, could not be preserved pure, but were embittered by petty competitions and worthlefs emulation. They were always jealous of the beauty of each other; of a quality to which folicitude can add nothing, and from which detraction can take nothing away. Many were in love with triflers like themfelves, and many fancied that they were in love when in truth they were only idle. Their affection was feldom fixed on fenfe or virtue, and therefore feldom ended but in vexation. Their grief, however, like their joy, was tranfient; every thing floated in their mind unconnected with the paft or future, fo that one defire eafily gave way to another, as a fecond ftone caft into the water effaces and confounds the circles of the firft.

With

With thefe girls fhe played as with
inoffenfive animals, and found them
proud of her countenance, and weary
of her company.

But her purpofe was to examine more
deeply, and her affability eafily perfuaded the hearts that were fwelling with forrow to difcharge their fecrets in her ear:
and thofe whom hope flattered, or profperity delighted, often courted her to
partake their pleafures.

The princefs and her brother commonly met in the evening in a private fummer-
houfe on the bank of the Nile, and re-
lated to each other the occurrences of the
day. As they were fitting together, the
princefs caft her eyes upon the river that
flowed before her. "Anfwer, faid fhe,
great

great father of waters, thou that rolleſt thy floods through eighty nations, to the invocations of the daughter of thy native king. Tell me if thou watereſt, through all thy courſe, a ſingle habitation from which thou doſt not hear the murmurs of complaint?"

"You are then, ſaid Raſſelas, not more ſuccefsful in private houſes than I have been in courts." "I have, ſince the laſt partition of our provinces, ſaid the princefs, enabled myſelf to enter familiarly into many families, where there was the faireſt ſhow of profperity and peace, and know not one houſe that is not haunted by ſome fiend that deſtroys its quiet.

"I

" I did not feek eafe among the poor, becaufe I concluded that there it could not be found. But I faw many poor whom I had fuppofed to live in affluence. Poverty has, in large cities, very different ap-pearances : it is often concealed in fplen-dour, and often in extravagance. It is the care of a very great part of man-kind to conceal their indigence from the reft : they fupport themfelves by tempo-rary expedients, and every day is loft in contriving for the morrow.

" This, however, was an evil, which, though frequent, I faw with lefs pain, becaufe I could relieve it. Yet fome have refufed my bounties; more offended with my quicknefs to detect their wants, than pleafed with my readinefs to fuccour them : and others, whofe exigencies com-pelled

pelled them to admit my kindnefs, have never been able to forgive their bene-factrefs. Many, however, have been fincerely grateful without the oftentation of gratitude, or the hope of other fa-vours."

End of the First Volume.